ARMAGEDDON:
PICK YOUR PLOT

ARMAGEDDON:
PICK YOUR PLOT

By AJ Lauer and Daniel Keidl
Frog & Lion Press, Boulder, Colorado

Frog & Lion Press
Boulder, Colorado

Cover and book design by Daniel Keidl.

First edition, December 2012.

ISBN-13: 978-0615715858
ISBN-10: 0615715850

ACKNOWLEDGMENTS

From Dan:
This book was an epic labor of love as a thank-you to my friends and family on the occasion of my birthday. May you all survive life by the skin of your teeth and have a book-worth of amazing tales to tell of it after!

From AJ:
Many thanks to Dan for being born, being awesome, and asking me to help create this disastrous adventure. Err... adventure of disasters. I hope you all enjoy your many deaths as much as we enjoyed subjecting you to them :)

Special Thanks to:
Ben Stephens, for insight and scratchy brown carpet. Alison Krautkramer and Chris Lauer for technical advice and being nice about AJ ignoring you while she wrote. Dan's Mom, for giving birth to him so he could do awesome things for his birthday every year! And thanks to Real World Disasters for inspiring fear and creativity in generations of humans.

THINGS TO LOOK FOR
WHILE READING
ARMAGEDDON: PICK YOUR PLOT!

Find all four indirect routes to the four Horsemen of the Apocalypse! They are the manifestations of each Horseman's specialty, and are related to the Martian Invasion, Global Thermonuclear War, the Superflu Pandemic, and Climate Change.

Find all three fiery deaths! They are Global Thermonuclear War, the Fire Hurricane, and the Solar Supernova.

Find all nine survival scenarios (where Elisabeth doesn't technically die, although she may wish she did).

Find all these, and you'll be pretty cool!

As a young child, you always were a bit of a mystery to everyone. While prune-wrinkled great-aunts would pinch your cheeks tenderly and laugh delightedly, "Oh, what a beautiful princess Elisabeth is!", you were always happy to join your dad and uncles in a pickup game of touch football in the backyard on Easter weekend. A child of diverse interests and passions, no one could ever put a definite label to you, and you liked it that way.

When you were only four years old, or so your parents tell you, you were playing the "Why?" game with your dad in the family room, and he was gamely playing along with you. You began with "Why is the sky blue?" and then gradually became more persistent as he got more elaborate with his answers, until pretty soon he was explaining molecular structure to you as you sat, awe-stricken, on the scratchy brown carpet. Mom and Dad shared a smile over your head and didn't think much more of it until a couple of days later, when your dad found you in your bedroom sitting on the floor with your toys, making admittedly inaccurate circle diagrams of neutrons, protons and electrons out of doll accessories and building blocks, and declaring each new arrangement to be a new molecule of great importance.

At seven your interest in mythology really blossomed, and you devoured whole volumes of Greek and Norse stories aimed at a grade-school reading level. Your mom hooked you on the legends of Arthurian England and Grimm's Fairy Tales by reading them to you at bedtime, and from then on you divided your time equally between exploring the sciences and finding and consuming ancient legends.

Every time something new caught your interest, you embraced it with passion and tenacity, and the advent of the Internet only broadened your ability to pursue your interests to new levels. You combed through old episodes of Star Trek while at the same time studying digital tomes of horticulture and unpublished papers on the mounting problem of dying bee populations.

When it came time for your first high-school science fair, your teachers were astounded and perplexed by the problem of how to grade your presentation on hypothetical models for ten-, eleven- and twelve-planet solar systems. Your physics teacher looked to your parents for help and was met only by two bemused and amiable expressions that said, "We don't know what to make of her either!"

No one could have guessed which way your life would lead, but here you are!

If you're on a high school field trip to the city observatory, turn to page 14.

If you're a college student pursuing dual majors in mathematics and theology, turn to page 32.

If you're an influential employee at a prestigious technology company, turn to page 38.

*O*h *Percy!* You never could resist those hazel eyes. It's time to gird your courage and get his attention. Appropriately enough, the elderly German tour guide stops the class before an exhibit about Pluto and its similarly-sized moon, Charon, co-orbiting each other in their long lonely path around the sun. You've long felt that was a romantic pairing. Maybe it's a sign?

Taking a deep breath, you skirt around the outside of the gaggle of your classmates and approach Percy from the side. Gently, you touch his elbow to get his attention.

"Percy..." you begin.

"Yes?" he turns his radiant face to yours, and in his eyes you see intelligence, talon-sharp and curious. And you see, too, recognition and interest. His eyes say it all, the glistening hazel communicates what words would only fumble around: his feelings for you are as ardent as yours are for him! Could this really be it? After waiting so long, finally you two have discovered your love for one another under the crossings of the stars...

Suddenly you begin to feel cold. Alarm leaps to Parzival's face and many of the students let out a gasp of shock. The whole museum's temperature appears to be dropping quickly! Looking outside through the large museum windows, you can see condensation forming on the surfaces of every building and freezing immediately in place. The blood in your veins begins to slow as the temperature of everything, everywhere, rapidly descends and equalizes.

After a moment's consideration, you realize what must be happening: It's the heat death of the universe! All the molecules are evening out in temperature. Potential energy is being negated as every form of energy becomes unable to transfer into any other form. The laws of thermodynamics necessarily presented this as a possibility, but no one ever imagined it would happen in their lifetimes!

You seize Percy's hands with the last capacity for movement that you can muster. *It's a truly amazing way to die, you think, and I wouldn't want to share it with anyone else.*

After a few moments more, there's no one left at all to share it with.

THE END.

Deciding to spit in the eye of every homely matron who ever warned her children not to stare into the sun directly, you crank the titanic telescope around to look directly towards the sun, the center of our solar system.

Eager to see sunspot activity or some other massive chemical reaction on the sun, you're alarmed to see a LOT of sunspot activity, all happening at once!

You knew that your beloved Sol was gonna die, you just mistakenly thought it was going to happen in 5 million years and that it would die like a burnt ember. Turns out it's dying now, and in a huge explosion. Nobody here should ever have lived to see this day come. One thing is for certain: as soon as the shockwave from the detonated star reaches the planet (see, those reruns of Star Trek WERE good for something), there won't be a planet left.

Resigned to your fate, you rush out of the observatory and back to the museum. Finding Percy Lewis, you seize his hand and haul him outside with you, receiving only token resistance.

From the parking lot, the two of you stand looking up into the sky as the light from the sun finally winks out, leaving the earth in darkness but for the man-made lights dotting its landscape. What feels like moments later, the front edge of the shockwave impacts the earth and you're both shoved to your backs against the crumbling asphalt of the parking lot, and then crushed into oblivion as the Earth, along with every celestial body of your solar system, is disintegrated into tiny shards and then sucked unceremoniously into the resulting black hole.

THE END.

The only thing worse than believing a preposterous hypothesis without proof would be denying the undeniable proof presented before you. Although the Planet X, Nibiru, cannot exist, nevertheless it does seem to be within observable distance of the Earth and moving past quickly.

Fascinatingly, this has an enormous impact on things like the icecaps and weather patterns and the orbit of the planet around the sun. The traumatic effects of Nibiru's passing leads to a wholesale shift in the axis of the earth. What was once polar is now equator and vice versa.

Knowing what you already know about how even tiny shifts in temperature in an area over the course of years can cause immeasurable damage and suffering to the species of plants and animals that live there, you find yourself unsurprised when the axis shift of the Earth results in complete climate change. Although you read about scientists' postulations that a polar shift like this must have happened many times in Earth's history, based on the polarity of magnetic lava on the ocean's floor, this marks the first time it's happened with the current batch of species on the planet's surface. Fragile, squishy humans are one of the first to succumb, yourself and your fragile, squishy crush Percy included.

THE END.

Heroically joining the ragtag resistance, a loyal and persistent group of the last holdouts of all the nations of the world, banded together under the common cause of independence for Earth, you quickly impress the resistance leadership with your bravery, accuracy and acumen. You work tirelessly to decode the mysteries underlying the alien weapons technology and stage daring raids on the Martians' supply installations.

After a time, you, young Elisabeth, become a kind of Joan of Arc figurehead for the resistance, and they rally around you. Miraculously Percy also survived the initial onslaught, and true to his namesake he defends you valiantly, as much as any knight of old. No matter how hard things get, you have each other, and you have the cause of freedom!

Unfortunately the Martians do not seem to respect the bit of notoriety you have gained since their arrival. You stumble upon an unhappy Martian sentry on a mission and shoot ineffectually at his powersuit a few times before he pulps you with his laserbeam eyes and hideous poisonous-gas breath. Glory!

THE END.

The rude tone of the student fades into the background and you feel the hum of a gentle choir of angels fill your ears.

Your unflinching compassion, self-acceptance and faith in God's plan leads Him to call you by name. First name.

ELISABETH.

"Yes, Lord?"

YOUR LIFE HAS BEEN A MIX OF TRIUMPHS AND TOILS, CHALLENGES AND TESTS, AND YOU HAVE BEEN FOUND WORTHY. YOUR FAITH IN ME AND YOUR LOVING HEART ARE A TESTAMENT TO MY PEOPLE.

"...Thank you, my God."

COME, BE WITH ME. SIT WITH ME AT MY TABLE; JOIN ME IN RAPTURE. AND BRING YOUR CUTE FRIEND TOO.

As you watch in awe, your body becomes insubstantial and your weak mortal shell is seared away, leaving a charred spot in the grass next to where Missy had also been sitting. Looking over to her, you can see her spirit smiling back at you, and you are both lifted up together into the heavens on beams of light.

THE END.

You decide not to take any chances. Since word has gotten out that things might not get better, little 'sustainable communities' have been popping up everywhere. These small cities tout open green spaces, community gardens and water recycling plants. The thought of drinking your own urine (or someone else's, no matter how filtered!) kind-of grosses you out, but in the end you decide it's worth it just to survive.

As the years pass you watch as every community in the state and many large ones in other countries waste away to nothing. Weather patterns are too erratic and no matter what anyone does there is just never enough water. Soon government ceases to function and common law rules. Your community becomes more strict about water and food, until only young children are allowed to eat more than once a day. Eventually you start to falter and the weaker among you begin to die.

One day you look out across the dusty plain and see a shrouded man on a black horse. Another bandit, you think. The community has already been robbed twice this week, so there is nothing left for him to steal.

Your eyes meet and you immediately feel yourself shriveling under his gaze. He bears a scale in one hand and appears to be weighing your worth. Finding you wanting, the Horseman of Famine turns his dark steed and trots on.

At his passing, you are overcome with a feeling of deep starvation, more poignant and painful than the daily hunger you have grown accustomed to. You fall to your knees, clutching your stomach.

Turn to page 43.

Your long-time crush on Percy Lewis started the day you met him in ninth grade. It was so obvious, honestly, that he was the most interesting boy in school. No wonder all the other girls have a thing for him too. He's cute, tall when most of the other boys aren't even your height, he enunciates well, he always seems comfortable and confident and, rumor has it, his real full first name is Parzival, making him the only boy at school named for an Arthurian knight and therefore, clearly to you, the best.

Today is the day everyone in your class has not-so-secretly been yearning towards for the last month: the senior class trip to the city observatory. Granted, very few of your peers have any interest in astronomy, but a trip to the observatory is a day without classes and a night in the city, and to students who have been cooped up in tan brick secondary-education walls for months, it is a very welcome reprieve.

The celestial sphere has been one of your myriad passions for a long time, as you've tracked eclipses of a dozen varieties, as well as meteors, comets... heck, anything that glows or spins and has to be viewed through a telescope. Once, you convinced your brother to drive you three towns over so you could be one of a score of similar enthusiasts combing a farmer's tilled field for bits of space-rock that crashed to earth in a meteorite the morning before. And it was worth it too; you found three separate pieces! They turned out to be types of rock that are also quite common on earth, but so what?

You follow the class around the observatory's museum wing as they're being lectured by an elderly and very German lady on the nuances of all sorts of astronomical displays that you've seen on your many prior visits. Your attention is divided between the face of Percy Lewis, as he raptly listens to the tour guide, and the hall that leads down to the observatory itself, which contains the titanic telescope that squints up into the sky, able to see things Copernicus would have wet himself to even imagine.

Since the eclipse you witnessed on May 20, 2012, the one that you feel was somehow especially significant, the universe seems less certain; the Earth seems more fragile. The observatory calls out to you now almost audibly. Maybe, just maybe, if you sneak in there before the demonstration for your whole class, you can get a good look out into the great unknown of outer space.

On the other hand, this is your last observatory trip; as seniors you won't be back this way together again. In fact most of you won't see each other much at all after graduation in a few weeks. Maybe the time is right to say something to Parzival, to let him know of your interest. The next time *die fraulein* stops the class group for any length of time, you could get his attention.

Do you...

Try to speak to Percy Lewis, turn to page 4.

Try to sneak into the observatory, turn to page 36.

Bide your time for a better opportunity, turn to page 26.

As a child you'd spent weeks studying various religions and mythologies, always fascinated to find out their concepts of the end of days. You know you've read about these events as signs and portents somewhere but can't quite believe your memory.

Rushing to the library you know so well, you and Missy find it nearly empty. You enter the special collections wing, step around security cordons and boldly walk into the utterly abandoned library-staff-only restricted section to find old tomes.

Hours of study of Bibles from ancient ages and other early theological texts lead you to a conclusion you could hardly believe, had you not seen the events occurring in the world outside the silent library. Mysterious events, unexplained attacks, sudden shortages, freak disappearances and widespread chaos... they can all be found attributed to one extraordinary event.

And it begins with the opening of four seals.

Turn to page 43.

Your background in mythology and history, and your voracious appetite for knowledge and theory, all contribute to give you a niggling sensation that there's something else at work here. After joining the resistance and traveling the Martian-ravaged landscapes of Earth in search of what else this might be, eventually you come across the horrifying truth.

One day, while advancing covertly across the countryside, you and your small ragged platoon come across a lone horseman in a field. He rides on a white horse, and in his hand is an archaic bow. Upon his head rests a crown soaked in blood. While he appears human, he has an unearthly glow about him.

Raising his bow to level and pulling back on the string, he slowly, almost languidly, begins to shoot down the members of your platoon. Though they fight back, guns a-blazing, nothing seems to touch the horseman. His horse stamps a hoof in the bloody earth and snorts. You flee to safety.

And suddenly it clicks. White horse, bow, crown. The sudden and brutal invasion of Earth at the hands of ruthless otherworlders. Though you can hardly believe it, you were in the presence of Conquest, a Horseman of the Apocalypse.

Turn to page 43.

Y ou and Eric decide that before you get too far into the obviously infested hospital, it would be best to stock up on some precious medical supplies - bandages, antibacterial medicines, powerful stunning agents. In the event that there really are zombies or something similar, you'd like to be able to at least put up a fight.

The ER is a cataclysm of unmade beds, dead and bleeding bodies, and hastily abandoned medical equipment. The two of you are careful to avoid touching any person or bodily fluid as you rush to the nurses' station.

Eric gestures to the carnage and says, "Dude, we've gotta clear out of here as soon as we get this stuff. If these things really are coming back to life, I don't want to be here to see it."

"But Dr. Saunders! She's one of my best friends! She could be dying somewhere.. We could save her!"

"Elisabeth, no. No, no, no. There's no way. Something is obviously going completely wrong here and we are not going further into this cesspit. Grab your meds, tell me what to take, and let's go."

You each grab a pillowcase from the closet (hopefully still disinfected - yikes!) and start dropping handfuls of medication and supplies into them. Just as both bags get filled to capacity someone knocks over a prep pan across the room. You start and both you and Eric turn to see a half-dressed, previously-human creature lumbering toward you. "RUN!!" you both shout and almost knock each other over in your rush to get out.

There are two more creatures near the reception desk but they are occupied with eating what you assume to be a recently deceased receptionist and don't notice you.

Careening out of the door, you rush to the car and heave a sigh of relief as you collapse into your seats.

With the doors locked, you head out of the parking lot toward Eric's father's house. He'd always thought the old man was crazy, but suddenly that 1950s bunker and gun collection don't look so bad. You call your staff to tell them to seek shelter, but can make no move to rescue them. It about to be man-eat-man out there and you're not going to take care of anyone but yourself.

THE END.

He told you it was only to be used in emergencies, and you can't imagine anything more classifiable as an emergency than the imminent destruction of the planet, so you pull out your vintage-style cellphone and jam your thumb on the "4" button until auto-dial starts to ring your father.

"Dad? DAD! Listen, it's a HUGE emergency!"

"What is it, Elisabeth? Are you hurt? What's..."

"No time, Dad. I'm at the observatory, and I've just seen a huge asteroid, hurtling towards us! It's the world-ender, Dad. You have to tell someone!"

While you've had many interests in your long career as a human being, crying "wolf" has never been one of them, and your Dad recognizes this. As you start to usher the old men out of the observatory and try to find some kind of fallout shelter or something to hole up in, he calls in a few favors with his old friends in the military to get on the line with someone very high up in the chain of command.

Then, as you try to get your dubious, and then

panicked classmates, (including Percy Lewis) into the shelter, a wing of F-16's screams through the sky above the city, breaking sound-barrier regulations as they race to release nuclear payloads at the huge rock heading towards the human race.

In the end they succeed, splintering the meteor into numerous fragments. It was too late before they even started, though; none of the smaller chunks divert course enough to avoid slamming into the Earth, and so the net result is more like a grapeshot impact on the northern hemisphere rather than a bullet colliding just on your exact location. Life as you know it ends, of course. Civilization collapses, the elderly, infirm and witless die off, and life becomes harsh as the world careens into a new ice age caused by what will forever be known as "Asteroid Elisabeth."

On the upside, you've never before had a better environment to experiment with what it must have been like to be a dinosaur. So there's that!

THE END.

The display has a frightful lot of information and conjecture about the changing perception of gravity from Isaac Newton onward, and in a footnote of one small section in the corner of the display, you read about the "Planet X" theory.

In short, some learned people have posited the notion that there may be another previously unseen planet in our solar system, one that has an extremely long and irregular orbit around the sun. If this mysterious Planet X, also known as Nibiru, has sufficient mass, its own gravitational pull might be sufficient to muck up the gravity of Earth like this for some amount of time. Especially if it's passing close by. This reminds you of the science project you did in grade school - all those hours studying how planets interact with one another in space suddenly feel particularly relevant.

Now what?

If you embrace this ridiculous notion whole-heartedly, turn to page 44.

If you look for other explanations in the display on gravity that might help to clear things up, turn to page 48.

If you reject this idea as outright ludicrous, turn to page 8.

It's not much, mining uranium ore and hauling porcelain for the overlords, but if you're lucky they'll give you food once a week!

THE END.

You decide both confronting Percy Lewis and trying to avoid the watchful eye of the tour guide long enough to escape are too risky just at the moment, so you tag along with your classmates and pretend you haven't heard everything a billion times before.

The elderly German woman stops the crowd before an informational display showing the effects and theoretical causes of gravity, and an awed silence falls on the group. Your jaw drops a little, too, as you realize that the spheres of the display, made of lead and other materials and intended to be grabbed and manipulated by curious children, appear to be floating in the air above your heads! Has the museum finally got enough money from a donor to start doing high-tech restorations of their aging exhibits?

That notion dies promptly as you realize that not just the spheres, but also your hair, the contents of the open-topped wastebaskets, and a number of other light objects appear to be defying gravity and floating about as if they owned the place! Giving a little push off the ground with your feet, you sail gently and slowly through the air for several yards before touching back down.

This is pretty wild, but what's causing it? you wonder openly to yourself. *Where to look for answers?*

Where indeed!

*To examine the display on gravity for clues,
turn to page 24.*

*To ask the elderly German tour guide woman,
turn to page 46.*

You decide to ignore all the messages waiting in your office, and instead to spend some time getting accustomed to the concept of being at work. Since the Generic-mart Party came into office, you've had some trouble being a dedicated employee. They've allowed companies to splash advertisements on everything, and have pushed their own brands into practically mandatory usage by taxing other companies to the brink of bankruptcy. Even toilet paper advertises that Generic-mart is "concerned with your bottom line," and you find this to be quite distracting. You go to the break room (the door says Generic-mart helps you "keep a handle on things") to have a doughnut ("there are no holes in our policies!") and some coffee ("help us perk up the economy!"). On the way back you stop in the bathroom to get some lotion ("Zandy Brandy scented lotion - like the Normans, drunk and with soft hands"). You've revelled in that brand's success since they actually do use brandy in their lotion and it never fails to leave you a little buzzed.

You enjoy your high from using the lotion and click on the TV as you enter your office. A mechanical sounding woman with advertisements flashing behind her head announces that they've just received word that several batches of Zandy Brandy lotion are being recalled due to some kind of fast-acting topical poison and that all use of their products should be immediately discontinued. Symptoms in most people include a violent rash on the area of application but some people could experience more serious symptoms including stroke and even death. Your jaw drops in disbelief as you sink into your chair and close your eyes, never to open them again.

THE END.

In alarm, you yank your head back from the telescope viewing lens.

"What's wrong, little lady?" the old astronomer begins to ask, but you shush him pertly and start to edge your way around the narrow side of the platform to get a better look at the lenses.

"Careful, miss! Come back from there; you might get hurt!" You ignore the protestations of the feeble old guys as you start to shimmy up the telescope's wide brass casing to the top.

Once you reach the top, you breathe heavily on the exposed objective lens and, using the cuff of your sleeve, you clean it off. "How does it look now?" you call down to the pack of astronomers, but when you glance down to them, their expressions, frozen in horror, confirm your worst fears.

On the bright side, perched at the very top of one of the largest telescopes in the northern hemisphere, you have an excellent view of every pore of the enormous asteroid as it crashes into the Earth.

No need to feel singled out, however. Though many of the people of Earth survive the initial impact of the unnamed asteroid, the subsequent ash cloud chokes out the remaining life on the planet and leaves it a dull lump of rock, hurtling through space.

THE END.

Your natural adaptability and ability to learn, coupled with your voracious desire for knowledge, make you a shoo-in for the institution of greater learning of your choice, and when it came right down to it you decide to make your move to New York City to attend Columbia University. The change of pace of the big city, and the history and lore of the university itself, which dated to before even the founding of the nation, are easily enough to keep your young blood pumping.

College life is about what you were led to expect, at first. You race through the breadth of classes – both available and required – with enthusiasm, making friends with professors and peers alike and spending far more than your share of time in the gorgeous library. Your transition to the college lifestyle is complete when the choice between doing more studying or hitting the town with your friends is settled by simply sleeping less.

And with your glowing eyes and eager smile and unmatched enthusiasm, it's no surprise that the men are quite taken with you. However, you never meet anyone that quite fit what you are looking for in a partner. Until you meet Missy.

By all accounts she is a lovely creature, yes, with olive skin and curly dark hair to match her eyes, and she smells of earth and leather in a way that you find simply intoxicating. What you find in Missy, though, is really a kinship of soul that you've never felt anywhere before. Being with her is so easy, it's almost like cheating. *Life shouldn't feel this good,* you think to yourself at the end of one of your many dates out with Missy. *I have more than my share of happiness now.*

With a similar lust for life and learning, Missy is your perfect complement, and together your studies and adventures reach new heights. Few people know of your relationship, but nevertheless you both know what you have is special. And as you push each other to greater scholastic heights and follow through on solemn oaths to do things like actually try base jumping for real, their opinions don't seem to matter. Even still, you know what you're doing is what many people, including those you respect, would consider very wrong.

One breathless Saturday morning in summer, you wake in your bed and wander into your living room to scramble an egg with green peppers. Missy is propped up on an elbow on your couch in her white nightclothes, eating a bowl of sugar loops and flipping through the news. "Reports are coming in of a huge unexplained sinkhole in lower Manhattan..." the news anchor rattles off, seeming agitated. **BLIP** goes the television as she changes the channel.

"Wait, go back; what was that?" you say abruptly.

"I dunno, thome hoaxth probabby," Missy says around a mouthful of cereal.

"Well go back; I want to listen!" you retort, and Missy complies, sticking her tongue out at you.

You join her on the couch and as you both sit and listen to the news, what you hear starts to astound and confuse you. Reports are coming in from all over that miraculous and terrifyingly inexplicable events are happening all over the globe.

Swarms of rats emerging from the sewers, devouring the contents of a grocery store and then disappearing, bright lights like fireworks driving cars and semis off of highways, eruptions of unknown volcanoes, rapidly rising and receding seas, undiagnosable illnesses and the like create a picture of truly unbelievable chaos, apparently striking world-wide.

Scientists try to offer explanations, but wind up throwing their hands up in the air. There are none, and as happens whenever there are no explanations, people turn to their religions.

What's your approach?

If you seek solace in Christianity from the bizarre events unfolding, turn to page 54.

If you set out to try to unravel the mystery for yourselves, turn to page 58.

"There are so many more important things in our immeasurable universe than the possible affections of one silly boy," you mutter to yourself as you take a judicious left turn. The rest of the class moves right, following the ancient German tour guide, and you duck behind a statue of Galileo until they're out of sight behind a collection of astrolabes.

As quickly as you can, stepping lightly with your toes and with arms out slightly from your body like a skulking spy in a James Bond movie, you skip around the cordon barriers and down the dim hallway toward the observatory proper.

Upon passing through the large wooden double-doors, you are startled to see that the observatory isn't empty; a number of aged astronomers appear to be setting up the giant-sized telescope for the upcoming presentation to your class.

One of them notices you, his wizened face lighting up. "Hello there, young lady, are you lost?"

"No sir, just wanted to see the telescope and I couldn't wait," you say. *That's pretty much true.*

"My dear, that's exactly the kind of curiosity that will take you far in life. Come come, would you like to see it? We're just lining it up now, looking for some interesting things to show your friends."

Would you ever! The kindly graybeard helps you up onto the viewing platform and shows you the workings of the telescope. "Now these two swivels control the x and y axis of the telescope, you see. Try them out, that's it. Is there anything you'd like to try to see?" You're sure you could have figured it out on your own, but he's being so nice that you decide not to make an issue of it.

What would you like to look for?

To look for asteroids, turn to page 41.

To stare directly at the sun, Sol, the origin point of our solar system, turn to page 6.

You tap your fingers on the steering wheel as the song "It's The End Of the World As We know It (And I Feel Fine)" by REM comes on. Something about the song's perky treatment of world-altering events has always entertained you. You've just returned from a week's vacation and the world feels much finer than it did when you left. You park in the driveway and as you walk into the condo you find that your neighbor has dutifully collected your mail and fed the cat. Samael winds around your ankles, her tail flicking the end of your skirt, and you pick her up to cuddle.

A quick glance at the mail shows that you haven't missed much. The bank is still misspelling your first name and your brother sent his annual belated birthday card. You filter out the junk, and the sad little remainder of the mail scatters as you toss it onto the side table to be dealt with later.

You pause for a moment to appreciate the time you took to clean the house before you left. There really is nothing like coming back to an immaculate home. It helps you keep the clarity of mind you gained on your vacation.

A quick push of a button orders pizza brought to your home and a movie queued on the TV.

You start laundry while you wait for the delivery guy to arrive. After a week of trying new things, filling up on a favorite food and getting back into your usual routine comforts you. Upon arrival of the pizza you sink into the couch and take in a movie you will probably forget all about by tomorrow.

The next morning you awake on the couch covered in pizza debris. You've always struggled a bit with jet lag, and the only thing to wake you was Samael's insistence upon being fed. You stretch groggily and for the first time find yourself thankful that when your workplace restructured they also began requiring uniforms.

Since the merger, you find the thought of going in to work to be rather daunting. Due to your wide-ranging interest in many of the sciences, in the merger they tasked you as overseer of each department's most influential research projects. They've given you added responsibilities and a nicer office, but the new building is large and sterile, and you are concerned about the company losing its focus with all these new departments to keep track of. One of your tasks is to keep tabs on all the things that are going on and since you've been out a week you'll have a lot to catch up on. But a job is a job, and while you are not actively engaged in doing the research yourself, at least you're still working in the sciences.

You walk into your office to find your phone lines lit up, three messages from your secretary, and your voicemail notification flashing. *Goodness, you think, a girl steps out of the office for a couple days and the whole world ends!*

Of course you know what the messages are; your coworkers are stunningly consistent with the manner in which they attempt to contact you. The climate guys are quite persistent with the phone calls - which has always entertained you since everything they do is on such a slow scale. Corporate buffoons, of course, insist on contacting you via your secretary; any other method lacks appropriate formality. And the science nerds pretty much live at the lab, so your voicemail almost certainly contains half-delirious jargon-filled messages from four in the morning.

Which do you want to take care of first?

Talk to the climate guys on the phone, turn to page 94.

Read your secretary's notes, turn to page 55.

Listen to your voicemail, turn to page 82.

Not moments after you start to slowly pan the telescope across the sky, you find what you were looking for. Actually you find a lot MORE than what you were looking for; a huge asteroid appears to be hurtling toward the Earth! On its present descent it will collide with the planet in less than an hour, surely ending life as we know it. How could this be happening?!

Is it just dust in the telescope lens? Why isn't anyone doing anything about this?! Someone needs to be warned!

What will you do?

To raise an alarm, turn to page 22.

To inspect the telescope carefully for flaws, turn to page 30.

As you scan the skies intently, looking for the source of the roaring noise, you see in the distance what looks like a cloud approaching rapidly, high up in the sky.

Only after the cloud grows closer to you realize that it isn't a cloud at all, at least not of the regular condensation stuff. This is a cloud of huge winged lizards, hundreds or thousands of them -- it's hard to tell at a distance -- clustered together and moving at incredible speed. You see a burst of occasional flame in the cloud.

"Dragons," you gasp.

As the horde of ancient and mythical creatures impossibly descends upon you and their dragonfire envelopes the land, you are forced to concede that it's probably the very coolest way that you could ever die.

THE END.   *...Cheater.*

You've finally put your finger on it; you know why the world's come to such a shocking and horrifying end.

The world at war, invaded from without and consuming itself from within, suffering terrible shortages and mass death, is the world in the throes of the terrible power of the unstoppable Four Horsemen of the Apocalypse.

According to the Book of Revelations, the Horsemen of Death, War, Conquest and Famine are harbingers of the end of days, and as you look at the state of the world, you can see their influence everywhere. Lesser events and mortal ambitions are merely their tools to sow the absolute end of mankind in the soil of the Earth that it has crawled and lived on.

Fires engulf the planet in its shuddering death. Indeed the end of the world has come, and Judgment Day is nigh. Nothing can stop the Horsemen's ride across the planet.

Not even you.

THE END.

The Earth's orbit of the sun is a surprisingly fragile thing when it gets pushed around by the gravity of this big bully planet. Now that you know what's going on, you're utterly unsurprised when the powerful gravity of Nibiru rips the planet Earth off of its traditional and long-established orbit around the sun, and sends it hurtling straight towards the center of the solar system.

As the planet Earth begins to burn up in the sun, you take some small spiteful consolation from the fact that the earth's gravity necessarily had some kind of impact on the orbit of the mysterious Planet X, although given the differences of the two planets' masses, that probably didn't faze it much.

THE END.

"Give me some time to consult with my colleagues, Congressman. I want to make sure I am giving you the most informed decision that I can."

"Ok, Elisabeth. But we go into meetings tomorrow, so I will need an answer from you right away in the morning."

You call Dr. Eastling and he tells you he is an expert on Climate change, not politics. It is your and the government's job to figure out how to persuade North Korea to abide by your rules.

Tossing and turning, you wonder what to tell the Congressman. Fitful sleep yields no answers, only a very vivid dream about a tall, malevolent man bearing a sword, astride a fiery red horse.

You wake in the morning to find that the International Committee did not wait for your counsel, that North Korea did not like their solution, and that humankind is now at war. You are haunted by the image of the man on the red horse, and an overwhelming sense of dread.

Turn to page 43.

Before you can open your mouth to speak, your question is answered by unfolding events.

As cylindrical ships careen towards the Earth's surface from outer space and begin to disgorge large, oil-brownish aliens wielding technologically advanced weapons and inhabiting sleek impenetrable battlesuits, you can't help but be impressed by the surgical effectiveness of the Martian military's campaign against Earth. Now, the fact that humankind has never been able to prove the existence of life on the red planet makes a disturbing amount of sense!

Of course they propagated the idea that Mars was a lifeless desert planet; would you let a population you were about to enslave, a population that has always disputed the possibility of your existence, know about you if you could help it? Idly you reflect on how appropriate it is that humans named Mars after the god of war, for war they have indeed brought to Earth, and utter conquest.

In the early hours of the war, while the news stations still function, it is revealed that the Martians used some kind of gravity engineering device to disrupt the normal gravity of Earth, leading to the malfunction of key elements of our planetary defense and infrastructure, allowing the invaders to steamroll through the militaries of the disparate Earth nations as they willed.

This and their supreme martial might demonstrate amply their technological superiority and their ruthlessness. At the same time, you have this nagging feeling that there might be larger forces at work here. The only question that remains is,

What are you going to do about it?

To surrender to the Martian war machine and hope for leniency, turn to page 25.

To join the battered resistance movement in driving the Martian invaders off the planet, turn to page 9.

To pursue your gut feeling about other forces at work, turn to page 18.

Unfortunately your attention is drawn back to the Planet X section of the gravity display. The theories about Nibiru mention that it would have to be a particularly enormous planet, though they don't mention why they've come to this conclusion.

They really need to cite their sources, you think to yourself, which would make your seventh-grade science teacher proud if only he knew.

It's a moot point, however. A quick jaunt outside of the museum and a glance up at the sky makes it plenty obvious that there IS a planet messing up the Earth's gravity. Unfortunately and far more seriously, the intruder planet appears to be also on a direct collision course. Like a meteor, Nibiru collides with the Earth. The metaphor is more appropriately used to describe the tiny Earth colliding with Nibiru, but either way, both planets are sundered and the broken and intermingled pieces of the two are swept into the asteroid belt, including you, your crush Percy, and all of civilization.

THE END.

Pancakes! The answer is pancakes! Suddenly it makes perfect sense!

Grabbing your kitty Samael, you leave the condo immediately and set off for North Dakota, stopping only long enough to pick up pancake batter and a handful of other supplies at the local grocer.

"With any luck, no one will need to die, Samay!" you exclaim cheerfully. Samael meows.

During the long drive, you have a while to reflect on what you'll find when you arrive at your destination, but even you couldn't predict the horrible, horrible truth that was in store for you.

Turn to page 43.

50

"You're right, damnit, you're right!" you cry out, anguished. Why is life so cruel, that the only person you've ever felt truly close to is a person you can't in good conscience choose to be with?

Missy looks at you alarmed, startled, and tears glisten in her eyes. "Elisabeth, I... we had each other..." she begins to speak, but you turn away and squeeze your wet eyes closed to avoid her gaze.

You here a soft *fwhump* noise and a rush of warm air, followed by the smell of smoke. Surprised and alarmed, you open your eyes and turn back to look where Missy had just been sitting.

Her clothes lie there, on the ground, in a circle of charred grass, as if she had simply vanished from out of them. Looking up, you and the rude student are struck dumb by the sight of numerous rays of light coming down from the heavens, illuminating the spot where Missy had just been, as well as many many others like it throughout the city. At the same time, aside from the rays of light, the world seems unnaturally darker. It seems that judgment has come, and you have been found wanting.

Life seems to go on after that day, painfully without Missy, although the violent and unexplainable events grow larger and more frequent. Too, things just don't have that "sparkle" anymore; you find yourself simply devoid of joy. Your weakness at the moment of truth has left you stranded in a world that is rapidly deteriorating past the point of no return, in the absence of its nicest folk.

In less time than you'd think, the world is tearing itself apart from the strife of the sinners, and from that fate, none survive.

THE END.

So calling a congressman isn't usually the most effective way to get things done, but you're an executive at a major company, remember? That's worth some clout! You call up Congressman Miner to have a chat and he naturally senses opportunity.

"Wait, so you're telling me we finally actually have evidence of climate change? This drought stuff isn't just a passing thing? Forward me that report. This is something I want to take seriously."

Though you can tell the Congressman is only doing this for his own benefit, you decide to forward him the report. Some progress is better than none, and he sits on a couple important government committees, so he may as well have at it.

He does gain the ear of other policy makers and a worldwide frenzy soon starts as some countries adopt severe austerity measures and some have those measures imposed upon them. You are happy that the Congressman repeatedly calls you to see what your thoughts are on the policies and of course you speak often with Dr. Eastling to make sure your advice is well-founded.

One day Congressman Miner calls you and says, "Elisabeth, I've got a difficult decision to make, and I need your help. North Korea, in their perpetual obstinacy, refuses to adopt the international standards for austerity. I don't need to tell you that this is a delicate matter. North Korea is touchy and we did confirm their nuclear capabilities last year. We have a few options and I need to know your input."

Which do you advise him to do?

Send in a mediator, turn to page 78.

Further restrict trade with key players in the North Korean economy, turn to page 101.

Consult your resident climatologists, turn to page 45.

The Bible's full of talk about the end-times, the second coming, and whathaveyou. Even prominent theologians believe most of these are hyperbole and metaphor, but which ones are real?

As you and Missy enter the Christian chapel at Columbia, you find it already packed to overflowing with people, including students, professors and anyone off the street.

"This isn't going to get us anywhere, love," Missy whispers loudly in your ear, over the hubbub of murmuring, chanting and prayer. "There isn't even any room."

"If only it had ever been this busy before," you mutter back. "The bishop would have been ecstatic!"

"There's no atheist in a foxhole," quotes Missy as you turn around and exit the building.

There has to be something you can do now. But where to look?

If you look for somewhere to stop and listen to God, turn to page 56.

If you consult ancient texts about the Biblical armageddon, turn to page 17.

You decide to let the phone go to voicemail. Anything having to do with climate change can wait - it's not like the polar ice caps are going to melt all of a sudden. You pick up the messages, and in your secretary's neat handwriting find that your old college buddy Eric has called three times, wanting to talk about Hurricane Catherine.

Sometimes Eric calls about important things, and sometimes he calls about things that don't matter. But what you can always count on is that he will want to talk for a long time about whatever is going on. You just got in so are not quite sure you're ready for that in-depth of a conversation yet.

What do you do?

Ignore messages, spend some time dawdling, turn to page 28.

Ignore messages, stop to check in with your boss, turn to page 74.

Call Eric, turn to page 81.

Finding a quiet garden in a lesser-traveled part of campus, you and Missy sit down on the green and tenderly join hands as you try to block out the distractions of a world that is evidently going mad.

The noise of the city, the sound of distant explosions and people's cries and wails slowly fades to white as you take solace in each other's support and find a calm within yourselves. Only a handful of passers-by filter through this area of the garden. No divine voice calls out to you, though. No sign seems to be forthcoming. Nevertheless, the exercise of reaching out to God renews your spirit and makes you feel strong again.

Abruptly you're both shaken out of your meditation as a loud, abrasive voice yells to you from very close by. "HEY, YOU TWO! Stop that! Get away from each other."

Snapped out of your calm, you and Missy turn to face the voice. You see a young woman in crisp professional clothing with a handful of books and a backpack on her back, clearly some kind of student of the university. She stalks toward you with an angry stride as she continues to speak in an aggressive tone.

"*Your* kind are the very reason for this catastrophe! If you weren't sinning with each other every damn day, disregarding Biblical law, God would NOT be doing this to us all now. Your selfish and abominable *lifestyle choice* has angered Him!"

How do you respond?

If you tell the woman to go shove it, because you're staying with the one you love, turn to page 10.

If you repent your sinful *life with Missy, turn to page 50.*

Hastily clothed and emerging at a run from your apartment building, Missy and you make your way up Manhattan to the site of the reported sinkhole to look for clues. As always, you admire her pluck and courage and heck, her sheer stamina. As she glances back to you briefly, you can see she's thinking the same thing about you.

Finally you arrive at the sinkhole, which takes up the entire intersection of 1st Street near the St. Joseph's House. The number of people at the site is low as the ground is still shaking and the possibility of another sinkhole or a collapsing building seems entirely likely.

By unspoken agreement, you and Missy start to find hand- and foot-holds to work your way down the steep walls of the sinkhole to the base of it some hundred feet below you. Accustomed to working together, you help each other get down safely and start casting about for clues.

"Elisabeth, look!" exclaims Missy, pointing across the sinkhole's width to the other end. A group of very short and stout people, like dwarves, with big beards and bronze armor, are clustered around a wide stone double-door set in the wall. They spy you both at the same moment and, in a scramble of movement and piping of high-pitched voices, they tumble through the door and slam it closed as you and Missy run up.

"Excuse me, um, misters!" you call out at the door, and Missy raises an eyebrow.

"Misters?" she asks, archly.

"I don't know what to call them," you reply, shooting her a dark look.

"How about 'dwarves.' That's what they are," she says.

"Fine. Excuse me, DWARVES, please come out! I... we'd like to talk to you. We're friends."

From behind the heavy stone doors you hear a gravelly voice call out, "Go AWAY."

"Can you at least tell us what's happening?" shouts Missy, pleadingly.

After a moment's pause, the door opens a bare inch and you can see a beady white dwarf-eye looking up at you from the darkness. "Aye, lady. Ragnarök. The end of times." Just as suddenly, the door is slammed shut. There don't appear to be handles of any sort on the outside.

You and Missy turn to each other and stare. "Ragnarök?" Missy asks in a low monotone, looking at you intently. "The Norse myth?"

Myth indeed! What will you do?

*If you try to gain entry to the dwarves' hold,
turn to page 66.*

*If you climb back out of the sinkhole
to weigh your options, turn to page 70.*

It doesn't take long to realize you've made the wrong decision. You bump along with your eco-fueled ego in your eco-fueled vehicle and reuse every piece of plastic and glass you encounter, but it isn't enough.

You decided not to use the power of your position to help save the world, and now the planet is suffering for it. Within a couple years the entire Earth is consumed by famine. There's no way to eat all those glass bottles you've saved through the years, so you fall prey to the same fate as everyone else. Nice going, hotshot.

THE END.

The phone goes almost immediately to voicemail. You hear Eric, in a panicked voice, saying, "This is Eric, if you are getting this message, immediately seek shelter. Our theories were correct - a lightning strike has caused fire on the Gulf which was picked up by the inflow of hurricane Catherine. All Gulf-side communities should seek immediate shelter in concrete and non-flammable buildings. Seek shelter, I repeat, seek immediate shelter."

Cursing, you run to the hallway and hit the bunker alarm. It was built to protect from scientific catastrophes in your microbiology lab, so it has its own air supply and months worth of food. It's completely cement so you hope it will be safe enough.

Everyone runs into the bunker and drops of fire begin to rain from the sky just as you close the door and the emergency lights flicker on.

Days later, you exit the bunker. The building survived the hurricane but upon emerging you find a destroyed world. Fire burns as far as your eye can see, and the sky crawls with lightning through the smoky atmosphere. Much of the city has burned to the ground and looters are having their way with what few stores are left standing. There are helicopters flying about, but cell phones and landlines seem to both be out so you have no way to communicate with authorities. You instruct your employees to attempt to get home but for safety purposes, to make sure to return to the bunker by nightfall.

You did make it home to get a change of clothing and other supplies. There was relatively little damage to your apartment - gotta love those ancient cement buildings! Unfortunately, your cat Samael seems to have disappeared, but you trust her feline instincts to have saved her.

Considering that your city is a long way from the Gulf but still sustained such significant damage, you don't anticipate that help will be arriving soon. Locations that were more directly hit must have far worse damage than what you are seeing here, and will take precedence when assigning aid. So when you make it back to the bunker you begin to organize supplies and groups of people, preparing for a long wait. At the end of the day, only about half of the staff returns. Grateful for your ability to use the company's resources to help those that have returned, you cross your fingers, hope the missing are ok, and prepare a survival plan for those in your care.

THE END.

"Sorry Eric, we've got some of the best minds in the country here, and there's nothing saying this is some kind of major disaster. Maybe we'd benefit from a bit of competition, eh?"

"If you say so. Let me know when you change your mind, ok?" Eric says and hangs up the phone.

You turn to Dr. LeFevre and direct him to gather his team. "Alright. We need a solution and we need it fast. Contact the hospital and get some samples and for God's sake be careful, ok?"

Reports of more and more deaths file in over the hours. By mid-afternoon it is reported that a fourth of the US population has flu-like symptoms, and by day's end the number is approaching forty percent. Schools and public areas have announced closures and grocery stores everywhere are mobbed by Lysol-armed citizens wearing protective masks.

You contemplate calling Eric to see if they have made any progress but your ego does not allow it.

You drive home to your condo, being careful to disinfect your door handle and anything else before you touch it. You see obviously ill people scattered along the road and sidewalks everywhere. By the time you go to bed the news reports that the death toll is rising and there is no remedy in sight.

When you wake up in the morning you notice that your eyes are red and breathing is raspy. You don scrubs and a mask and head to the office, wishing to help but not wanting to risk getting others ill. Dr. LeFevre and his team have been up all night and eye you suspiciously when you enter, but allow you to help.

"The death toll is rising, Miss. Our systems just cannot handle this kind of virus, and we are not making progress. I am afraid there may be nothing we can do."

You nod dimly, mumble to him to keep you posted and head up to your office. You collapse in your leather chair and flip on the TV. You struggle to listen as a reporter is saying, "The reported death toll in this horrifying outbreak reached one million this morning. Stores are being bought clean out as panicked consumers stock up ... to quarantine themselves away from others who may be contaminated. Scientists seem baffled ... and experts' ... advice is to hunker down..."

THE END.

"Hey, dwarves! Let us in there with you!" you call out to the door. Silence only responds.

"What Elisabeth means is," enunciates Missy, "could you grant us passage, please? We wish to enter your glorious hall. We seek sanctuary with you."

The dwarves, if any are still listening behind the door, do not reply. As you and Missy wait there, glancing at each other, you can hear a low rumbling. It's followed almost immediately by the wail of an emergency siren from above. Suddenly alarmed, you attempt to scale the walls of the sinkhole back to New York City street level, but the rumbling of the earth increases and climbing becomes impossible.

Suddenly the source of the low rumbling becomes clear: water starts to rush into the sinkhole from all sides! Did the ocean level suddenly rise? Is Manhattan itself sinking beneath the waves?! Alarm turns to panic as you and Missy realize your chances at survival are becoming remote. You turn as one and pound on the stone double-door with all your might.

"Mister dwarves, please! Let us in!" you call out, as the water quickly fills in the sinkhole to your knees, waists, and chests.

"Please! We're begging you!" gasps Missy as the water reaches your necks.

The last thing you hear, before a great wave strikes the streets of Manhattan and pulls you under for good, is the forlorn voice of a dwarf, saying slowly, matter-of-factly, "Sorry, there's just not enough mead to go around."

THE END.

Eric answers the phone on the first ring, "Took you damn long enough! Where have you been?"

"I was on vacation this weekend. What's going on, Eric?"

"You need to get your people into the bunker. Lightning from the outer bands of Catherine has lit the Gulf oil spill on fire! It's causing greater inflow and Catherine is expanding exponentially. She's pulling up the fire and it's mixing into the hurricane with oily water that's coming up from the Gulf."

"Eric, we've been over this. The 'firecane' is bullcrap. Water and oil can't get pulled up into the hurricane like that. And besides, she's headed for Florida. That's hundreds of miles away from here. I'm not going to scare all my employees by herding them into the bunker."

"But, it's real! I'm telling you my guys can see it on the radar. You're on the edge now but it's growing rapidly, uncontrollably, and you're definitely in its path!"

"Eric, I have more important things to do. I'll talk to you later."

You hang up the phone and walk over to the window. Sighing, you look out over the horizon, and blink. *What...? It's well past sunrise, why is the horizon glowing?* You curse loudly, and cast about trying to figure out what to do, as fire begins to rain from the sky. There's no way to get everyone into the bunker before being hit by the oncoming wave of incineration.

You hit the alarm, hoping that some people can get in to safety. With no time to make it to the bunker yourself, you return to the window as the first red-hot torrents of wind strike the edge of the compound and sweep over you. It's pretty, in a deadly, watching-the-world-end-in-front-of-you, kind of way.

THE END.

As you scale the sinkhole back to street level, the earth begins to rumble more and more violently. You're both lucky to have some experience in rock climbing, as you make it to the top of the wall and heave yourselves over onto the pavement once again.

Gasping for breath, you're not prepared for what you behold before you: A giant wolf the size of a two-story building, standing alert with four paws planted apart, filling the whole of 1st Street and growling menacingly. Fire flickers in his eyes and steam rises in billows out of his nostrils. Clearly worked up, its huge chest rumbles in a ear-shattering rumble of a growl and it bares its teeth, looking about it wildly.

"Elisabeth, if this is Ragnarök, does that make that THING Fenrir?" asks Missy.

"Fenrir? Gosh... I suppose so. Can this be real? Am I...? I'm not dreaming," you sputter out.

The wolf-creature's growl cranks up a notch as it spies its prey, a large man in a winged helm, hoisting a great hammer on his shoulder as he strolls toward you and Missy.

As the wolf stiffens and the man approaches you, you can see that his eyes are unearthly, filled with a sparkling white light, like Roman candles, and no pupils to speak of. The deific man reaches you, extending a hand to be shaken. "Greetings, humans. My name is Thor, and I am a god. If you would kindly move a ways away, I have some business with this creature who devoured my father." He gestures with the hammer towards the steaming Fenrir.

Struck speechless, Missy and yourself step aside as the self-styled god, fully seven feet tall, strides past in jangling armor of what look like serpent scales and shifts his grip on his hammer, taking it in both hands as he faces the beast.

"Oh, one more thing," he calls out. "If I know my prophecy, and I do, you beautiful ladies had best start looking for a boat!"

Startled to action by his words, you start to run again, this time toward the harbor. Though the water boils and churns and everyone has evacuated to higher ground, Thor's commanding words still echo in your ears and you and Missy select a small sailboat with a cabin and an outboard backup motor. Your semesters participating in the water activities available at

Columbia come in handy as you prep the boat, but even then you're only barely ready to loose the moorings when you hear the death-howl of a great beast and a loud crack of thunder in the distance.

"Looks like Thor's business is done," says Missy, wide-eyed.

Less than a minute later, as you steer the boat out into deeper water, a loud shaking and rumbling fills your ears as, to your horror, the island of Manhattan sinks under the waves. Your little ship tosses and turns but doesn't capsize under your skilled hands. The water level continues to rise, or the earth continues to sink, until nothing can be seen of the city of New York, not even the tallest spires of the skyscrapers.

After several days of floating about, looking fruitlessly for land and subsisting on the bare rations of the sailboat's larder, the water begins to recede. Finally the land becomes visible again, but every remnant of civilization appears to have vanished with the tides.

"No people, no buildings... nothing is left," you gasp.

"Surely there are SOME people, somewhere," pipes up Missy, your stalwart companion. "We just have to find them."

"The Norse were right," you say. "Ragnarök was real. And the world has been born anew."

THE END.

You decide that rather than check on any of your messages, you might be better served by peeking in to speak to your boss. He always has the big-picture perspective and might be able to warn you about what's up before you deal with your phone. You knock to enter his office and are surprised to find what looks like a dunk tank in his office.

He looks up as you enter and says, "Well, you're just in time to find out the big news! Remember how I mentioned at the staff meeting before you left that we are going to be putting some new policies in place to help our employees with work-life balance?"

"Uh, uh-huh," you manage to make out before he continues.

"Well, I just got final word from the boss that we're all going to start using these sustenance-machines! See, it's actually pretty neat; you just climb into this tank and they hook you up to the machine..." He loops his arm around a connection port of some kind to demonstrate. "And it takes care of everything you need. We'll never have to go home or deal with a commute ever again! Your machine will be arriving in about an hour. The building has just been locked down, so there's no need to try to get home. I suggest you call your loved ones and let them know that if they want to interface with you they'll have to find your mind on our extra-net. Here is your identity and passcode. Hurry along. You are scheduled for hookup in two hours."

You have no option but to hook up to the machine. You go up to your office, call your mother and siblings, and tidy up. Don't want to leave a mess!

THE END.

The elevator music switches to a tropical mix as you head to the basement. The new radio system that changes the music depending on where you are headed is just about the best thing your company has ever done. You suppose they chose tropical for the Biology floor due to the tropics' biodiversity.

Just as you exit the elevator your cell rings. It is Eric, an old classmate. You were competitors all through school and that didn't change when you got into the corporate world. You went to work for separate companies, doing slightly different things; Eric is still more involved in the sciences, whereas you chose the management track. But you have found it beneficial to keep in touch, especially when there is something important going down. You have other things to worry about, so let the phone go to voicemail. You'll call him back later.

Dr. LeFevre greets you at his office door, looking frazzled. "Miss Elisabeth, I am so glad you came down. We've had a rash of cases of flu, in several major cities. But Miss, it's not spreading in the normal way. It's very fast. The hospitals are overwhelmed, almost overnight. I am at a loss for what to do. Perhaps if we could get a sample or a patient we could work on a vaccine or medication, but it is spreading so quickly!"

As Dr. LeFevre finishes talking, your cell phone rings again. It is Eric. You excuse yourself and answer, "Eric, I'm kind of busy. What do you want?"

"Elisabeth! There's a flu spreading through all the major cities in a tri-state area. It's faster than anything I've ever seen. High fevers, people's hearts stopping, massive dehydration.. We've got to do something to stop it. We need to combine forces to attack this thing."

You consider the fact that both Dr. LeFevre and Eric are concerned about this flu and need to make a decision about what course to take. On the one hand, if it really is that bad, it might be good to combine forces with Eric. On the other hand, you sometimes wonder if Eric isn't trying to steal some of your tech.

What do you do?

Combine forces and work with Eric to find a cure for the flu, turn to page 84.

Tell Dr. LeFevre to work with his staff to find a cure, turn to page 64.

Call in another colleague for a consult, turn to page 90.

But wait, there appears to be a glitch in the computer system! Turn to page 80.

"Sir, I think it would be best to send in a mediator. You know the North Koreans are picky about how the world speaks to them, and also that they do best when they're spoken to directly. Maybe make sure you send some attractive female agents as eye candy for the Dear Leader, and .. perhaps it would be wise to deploy anti-missile cruisers, just in case?"

"You are absolutely right, Elisabeth. I will advise the Committee to do so. Thank you for your counsel."

The next day you get word that a mediator has been sent to North Korea. You know that what is not being said is that the United States is also preparing for war. After three days of negotiation the mediator emerges with an unhappy look on his face and the world knows that North Korea has yet again refused the world's entreaties to help save the planet Earth. Within an hour of the mediator's plane taking off, newscasters begin to make panicked reports - the mediator's plane has been shot down and word is that North Korea has armed its nuclear missiles.

You wonder what happened in the mediation but hope that the Congressman took your advice about the missile defense system. It soon becomes evident that they did, and it is a good thing. North Korea has shot several nuclear missiles at the United States, Japan and the United Kingdom. The missile defense system destroys two of the missiles but is not able to prevent three from striking major cities. New York, Miami and Omaha are destroyed and the country is soon covered in ash clouds and acid rain. Within two years nuclear winter begins to take hold and every person still alive is housed below ground, required to take massive doses of antiradiation medication.

Due to the prior famine, what little rations countries were able to stock up will not hold long and you and your colleagues know you are living on borrowed time.

THE END.

You glance at the shared workstation and suddenly notice that the screen is snowy, like an old-timey CRT television late at night when stations weren't broadcasting. *Strange, that's a plasma monitor... I didn't even know it could do that!* Abruptly the screen clarifies and flashes to the image of a man riding through a field on a horse. His light-colored steed plods on as the man appears to be content to soak in his surroundings.

Then you notice that all the monitors in all the workstations appear to be showing this video. Is it some kind of computer virus?

At any rate, it's quite picturesque, until the field begins to die around him. No, not just the field. Everything. You can see a dead bunny rabbit too! Around the rider life appears to be growing rapidly diseased, and perishing within moments.

You are reminded about a mythic story of horsemen, and suddenly, like a blow to the head, you are struck with the truth. You are gazing upon Death, the end of all, the rider of pestilence, a biblical Horseman of the Apocalypse in the flesh.

Turn to page 43.

Eric is an old college classmate. You were competitors all through school and that didn't change when you got into the corporate world. You went to work for separate companies, doing slightly different things; Eric is still more involved in the sciences, whereas you got thrown into the management track when your small firm merged with the research powerhouse that is now your employer. But you have on occasion found it beneficial to keep in touch, especially when there's something important going down.

The National Hurricane Center has not forecast Catherine to make landfall anywhere near your location, but you decide to call Eric to find out what is going on, anyway. If it's bad enough to necessitate three phone calls it's probably worth calling him back.

Your office phone continues to ring, so you use your cell to call Eric.

If you call and:

Get Eric's voicemail, turn to page 62.

Speak to Eric, turn to page 68.

You decide that whoever is calling persistently can wait, as can whoever left messages with your secretary. If something is important enough to warrant a voicemail, it is worth listening to sooner than later. You enter your passcode and the computerized voice tells you that you have two messages.

The first is from a guy named Claude down in computer engineering: "Hey lady! So you know the nanotechnology project I've been working on? It works! I can't believe it but it works! Umm but I seem to have a bit of a problem, and might need some extra dough to fix it. Can you come down so I can show you what's up? Oh umm. It's 3:30am, so come in as soon as you get in, in case it can't actually self-sustain. Thanks!"

The second message is from Dr. Christophe LeFevre down in biology: "Good morning, Miss Elisabeth. This is Dr. LeFevre. Please, miss, as soon as you get in, we need your assistance. We have noted a viral anomaly and I am concerned about its impact. Please come help as soon as possible. Thank you, miss."

It seems that your morning will be spent in the science labs and everyone else's issues will have to wait. You head to the elevator and hesitate. Whose issue is more important?

Which floor do you visit?

Right! The nanobots! You'd read Claude's reports on the project with interest and feel a little rush of excitement for his success. To check them out, push the button for the fourth floor and turn to page 97.

Hmm... A viral anomaly worthy of concern? Better get down to the Biology lab; turn to page 76.

"Ok, Eric. Let's see what we can do. Have your best people in the room for a video conference call in half an hour and I will do the same. Hopefully we can knock this thing out before it gets too much worse."

You gather your best science minds and get the video conference going within twenty minutes. In that time you receive reports that the flu has begun to hit schools and nursing homes, hitting the weakest first. You also hear that it's spreading to smaller cities and towns, many of which are grossly under-equipped to handle major medical emergencies.

You turn on the conference call and the first thing Eric says is, "Elisabeth, it's man made. This isn't a natural occurrence; someone engineered this thing. Hang on, I'll send you our file."

A murmur passes through your staff and Dr. LeFevre says, "If it is spreading this quickly and it is a man-made virus, we need to start quarantining. I will speak to my brother at the CDC and see what can be done to start that process."

You and your staff review the file and concur that the virus is not naturally occurring. Several staff disappear to start to work on medication. You send a message to other offices telling them to go into quarantine mode.

You make an announcement over the intercom, "Your attention please. A major flu epidemic has been reported and is spreading beyond control in most major cities across the country. Its symptoms include high fever and heart attack and in many cases it results in death within twenty-four hours. We are working with the best minds in the country to come up with a remedy, but hold little hope that we will be able to solve the problem in time to prevent widespread deaths. This building will go into lock down in thirty minutes. You are free to leave to seek out family, but we suggest that you remain inside and join the rest of the staff in the bunker to avoid contamination. If you choose to leave the building you will not be allowed to return under any circumstances."

You then hit the bunker alarm and enter your code to open the heavy door.

The flu works its way through the entire population of the US within four days, resulting in the death of tens of millions of people and the incapacitation of millions more. You and seventy-five of your staff survive, but are not able to come up with a cure for the mysterious disease. Most of you lose your entire families in the pandemic and leave the bunker to find that only a handful of humanity has survived.

THE END.

You decide to head straight to the morgue to find out what is really going on. Having been friends with Saunders for many years, you know there is a back entrance that goes fairly directly to the morgue door, so you head there. You were obsessed with horror films for a couple months as a kid, and thus as an adult entering any building through the rear entrance gives you the creeps. You look about for something to use as protection and notice a heavy pipe fortuitously sitting near the entrance. You grab it in an effort to equip yourself in case you need defense.

The morgue is almost deathly quiet. Its smell of disinfectant is tinged with decay, which makes all the surfaces seem a little less white. You hear indistinct moaning and brace yourselves before turning a corner. "Saunders!" you shout as you recognize your friend, "Are you ok? We were so worried!"

Dr. Saunders stirs, and before you get close enough to touch her she sits up shakily. You know something isn't right. Her usually bright eyes have gone dull and her face lacks any expression when she sees you.

Your realize your fears were correct, and you immediately steer Eric toward the entrance to the morgue. As you approach the door, three more zombies come around the corner with a *shuffle-shuffle-thunk-thunk-shuffle* as they move quickly in your direction. You fumble with the code on the door, and your heart races as they make headway down the hall. You turn to focus, pipe in right hand, left hand on the combination lock. Eric stands as if paralyzed by fear, unable to move, as the creatures move closer.

"Got it!!" you shout as the lock makes a satisfying *shunk* noise and opens. You push the terrified Eric in to safety.

Just then one of the undead grabs ahold of your arm and sinks his teeth in, lancing your arm with a pain like a set of sharpened ginsu knives, tearing loose a patch of flesh before you wrestle yourself away. Within moments your mind grows foggy and the color grays out of the world around you, though you do your best not to faint. You slam the door shut and bolt it and then lean your back against it, exhausted, in pain and shock, still feeling the grip of the zombie against your arm.

You cast a desperate look at Eric, who has not yet noticed that you've been bitten. *Will I turn now? Am I becoming one of them? When Ghandi said,*

"Be the change you want to see in the world," I don't think this is how he meant it.

You stare at Eric and see the panic grow in his eyes as he notices your arm. As your vision turns red, you have one last conscious thought: *He always did have a delicious brain...*

THE END.

"You know what, Eric - I have another friend who is a virologist over at the hospital. Let me call her and see what she knows about this, ok? I'll get back to you."

"Sounds good. Keep me posted!"

You dial another college friend, Dr. Saunders, and she picks up almost immediately, "Hi! Got a shitstorm here, what's up?"

"Well, that's what I was calling about. Our guys noted the rapid spread of this flu thing and were wondering if you know anything, and also if there's anything we can do to help."

"We've got people coming in every minute. The ER is overwhelmed and we've already had four deaths this morning. People come in and seem as though they've just got the flu, then suddenly they've got a raging fever. Two of the four we lost actually had their hearts explode. I've never seen anything like it. I can send you some tissue samples with the afternoon courier if you like. The more people working on this the better. I'll let you know if we have any breakthroughs here, but I've gotta run for now."

She hangs up and you turn to Dr. LeFevre and his team. "Gear up, folks. I want every bit of this place as clean as it can get. I don't want any chance of even one of these bugs sticking around after we're done with this. I'll call Eric and let him know we've got tissue samples coming. Be prepared for him to bring some of his guys over to check it out."

You call Eric back and he promises to bring a team over after lunch. They arrive just as your team finishes eating and the scientists immediately begin sharing theories. "Just like the good ol' days, eh?" Eric says, "Remember the hours we'd spend in the labs?"

"Yeah, I remember - you talking about yourself, me working, you getting credit for my work..."

"Hey! That's not fair! I did my share! And it paid off for both of us in the end, anyway. Here we are, running the largest facilities in the city, working on a major epidemic, and you're worried about sophomore lab class." He shakes his head, "So typical of you Elisabeth, can't let anything go."

LeFevre walks over, "Miss Elisabeth, the tissue samples are here. We should begin our analyses."

Grateful to have gotten out of that conversation, you give the team permission to look at the samples and you and Eric go to the projection wall to observe their results. An hour into the analysis you get a call from Dr. Saunders, "Elisabeth! Any progress? We've had fifteen deaths since we spoke. I'm headed down to do more autopsies now. There has to be something we can figure out. Hang on a sec, gotta unlock the door."

You hear several beeps as Saunders enters her passcode, and hear her curse when she opens the heavy door. "There's... huh... Where's...? MacMillan, you're...? Where'd the... Why is the sheet on the floor? Oh. Oh! Oh GOD! Elisabeth! They're... ahh!!"

You hear a shuffling noise and Dr. Saunders' phone drops to the floor. You hear a muffled moan. It almost sounds like someone says something about a brain, and you hear a crunch as the phone goes dead.

You turn to Eric, "We need to get down there, NOW."

You run to the intercom for the team working on the samples and say, "Sorry guys, you're going to have to stay in there. There's an emergency at the hospital and we can't let you break quarantine in case of infection." You hit the emergency lock button amid the startled noises coming from the lab team, and run down to the car pool, dragging Eric with you.

Dead bodies lay all along the road leading up to the hospital. *So many people didn't even make it there!* You park in the closest spot to the door and debate about what your course of action should be.

Do you,

Go to the morgue to try to find Saunders?
Turn to page 87.

Head to the ER to stock up on supplies
before doing anything else? Turn to page 20.

"Ok, ok. I'll answer!" You say as you pick up the phone. You've always felt a little bad for the climate guys; they don't get much respect and are generally considered to be little more than hoarders of data.

"Oh so you finally pick up, huh? Took long enough." You sigh as you hear Dr. Eastling's voice on the other end. With the new government he got pulled into the private sector and has always been unhappy about being taken away from his pet projects. You've never found him to be particularly pleasant but there is obviously something going on so you try to sound upbeat.

"Good morning Dr. Eastling! How can I help you today?"

"Well, Elisabeth, as you know, due to my connections at NCDC we have access to all their information including reports dating as far back as 1880. I've been running a multi-tier model to analyze climate data and just last night I was able to run my first full predictive analysis of worldwide climatological trends. My system said, unequivocally, that the drought in Africa is a harbinger of future catastrophe. We need to act now to save water and get other countries to work with us to slow these climate changes. If we don't, drought and flooding will be upon us."

You sigh again. This is the kind of stuff environmentalists are always on about. You're surprised to hear it from Dr. Eastling since climatologists don't generally operate on this timescale. However you are not one to panic and decide to try to calm him. "Dr. Eastling, why don't you put together a thorough report and submit it for review. I don't know enough about climate change to be of much use here, but your colleagues might be able to help us determine an appropriate course of action."

"That is a good point, Elisabeth. You don't know enough to be useful here. I am sorry for wasting your time. I will bring this to my colleagues."

"Thank you, Dr. Eastling. Keep me posted on what everyone thinks."

A year passes and you hear little from the Climatology Department. The drought in Africa has been on for six months and millions are starving. Meanwhile parts of Russia and Europe are flooding, causing those areas to lose their crops. Even the American 'breadbasket' has gone dry and citizens must tighten their belts as the country dips into reserves and food prices skyrocket.

You contact Dr. Eastling and the information in his report is persuasive: the climate has changed and we ignored the warning signs too long to be able to save ourselves.

What do you do?

Work with your government colleagues to campaign for greener lifestyles in an effort to slow the decline; turn to page 89.

Contact your congressman to tell him the government should do something; go to page 52.

Do nothing but vow to live in a more eco-friendly fashion; turn to page 61.

Move to a 'sustainable community' which touts its self-sufficiency and environmentally friendly practices; turn to page 12.

You push the button for the fourth floor and tap your foot to the music. It's gotten much better since they changed the station from the old elevator music to something topical depending on the floor you are headed. In this instance it is electronica with a perky beat. Not bad.

You exit the elevator and turn left, and stop short as you are surprised to find what look to be hordes of small grey bugs covering the walls. They seem attracted to your steel-toed boots and as you attempt to shake them off you hear Claude's voice as he comes running down the hall. "My self-replicating nanobots! They are self-replicating! They're converting every molecule into clones of themselves! The overrides aren't working; I can't control them! They'll eat you alive! Get them off your boots and get out of here!"

You try to brush them off your boots but each one you touch latches onto your bare skin and cannot be detached. Within moments there are millions swarming over you and you find yourself staggering to the ground, unable to control your muscles. The last thing you comprehend is that the floor seems to be turning to a grey mush beneath you, and you sink into oblivion as your flesh becomes one with the robots dissolving the floor. With nothing to stop the self-replication process, in short order the entire planet Earth follows suit.

THE END.

You call a colleague in the Department of Agriculture and work with her to put together a committee to help people understand the plight of the Earth. The committee assembles a series of advertisements and children's programs designed to teach people about how to live more sustainably and, ultimately, how to survive should the droughts continue. The group gets rights to a classic puppet character and revives his old saying, "It's not easy being green" in an effort to appeal to a broad audience.

Many people respect the goals set by the program and follow its guidelines but it is soon clear that this will not be enough. The government enforces austerity measures and even that is not sufficient to keep everyone fed and healthy. Soon, coalitions form to secure certain communities against worldwide famine. Due to your position in the company and your scientific knowledge you are one of the privileged few allowed into such a community. However despite your position you are not granted extra rights or food and eventually must get accustomed to subsistence living while you watch thousands of people across the world die.

You continue to work with your colleagues in an effort to slow the disastrous climate change. You are alive but as your waist shrinks, so does your hope for the planet.

THE END.

"I think you should talk to China and Cuba and see if you can further restrict North Korea's ability to trade with the outside world. Embargoes have proven effective when dealing with other countries, and we know that North Korea is not self-sufficient enough to feed its people as is. If they care about their countrymen at all, they will have to sign on."

"You're a tough woman, Elisabeth. I sometimes wonder if you didn't go into the wrong field."

"Well, sir. I look at facts. And the fact is that our world is dying and if we don't all do our best to save it, we aren't going to last much longer."

After just one month of the embargoes, word arrives from North Korea that its citizens are getting desperate. The Committee holds out, with hope that its impoverished citizens' plight will convince the country to adopt the measures. Soon a grainy video is leaked. It is a North Korean scientist. He says that his family is dying, he is forced to work inhumane hours in an effort to develop weapons to use against the West, and that if something doesn't change soon he will launch the weapons himself.

International leaders decide that due to lack of verifiable credibility of the source, they cannot bend to the threat. Even North Korea declines knowledge of the identity of the worker, citing the grainy picture as making identification impossible. The day after this decision becomes public another video is released.

The man simply says, "Tell your children you love them."

Two hours later five missiles shoot toward each of the continents. Unprepared and unable to predict where the scientist will send the weapons, no country's missile defense system is able to engage in time to prevent major damage. Shortly after, a gigantic nuclear bomb rocks the entire Korean peninsula. It sends shockwaves through Asia and its vibrations trigger earthquakes along the Western edge of the Pacific Ocean. These in turn create a massive tsunami which hurtles toward North and South America. The nuclear fallout kills millions of people across every continent and causes irreversible radiation damage in those who live. You are one of the unfortunate ones whose body decays rapidly in the face of radiation poisoning. You hang your head over the toilet to vomit again and again, and die praying to the porcelain gods.

THE END.

ABOUT THE AUTHORS

Dan Keidl is a graphic designer and a truly rad dude. He was born and raised in Rochester, Minnesota. He now resides in Madison, Wisconsin where the sun always shines and delicious candy sprouts from every surface! All of the people who are his friends are among the best of folks. At this moment he is liable to be elbow-deep in some insane project. Oh and I'm handsome.

AJ Lauer works in Higher Education and Student Affairs and maintains a healthy reading and writing addiction. She lives near Boulder, Colorado where the Flatirons beckon and hippies sprout from every surface. She keeps a blog at *frodofrog.blogspot.com*. If you survive the book you should stop by to say hi!